Kassondra 3

D ALAN PAULY

iUniverse®

KASSONDRA 3

iUniverse books may be ordered through booksellers or by contacting:

iUniverse
1663 Liberty Drive
Bloomington, IN 47403
www.iuniverse.com
1-800-Authors (1-800-288-4677)

ISBN: 978-1-6632-0103-4 (sc)
ISBN: 978-1-6632-0102-7 (e)

Print information available on the last page.

iUniverse rev. date: 05/21/2020

I dedicate Kassondra 3 to my loving wife Rebecca of 51 great full years

Plot Synopsis

The destiny of a person is connected not only with those
things he, himself, created and does, but also with what
happened to his soul in previous incarnations.
...One's existence is therefore continuity, the sustaining
of a certain fundamental rise to the
surface which does not seem to belong to the present.

-Rabbi Steinsaltz-

$\mathcal{R}$ebecca Marshall is a widowed mother of two, living in a small town in Colorado.

Her major concern is getting through another day financially and emotionally with her two children.

But centuries away, in a primitive country besieged by an evil curse, forces are at work to draw Rebecca back to her destiny...a destiny that has followed her through countless incarnations and is now demanding to be fulfilled.

Rebecca has experienced being taken back through time to the period when she was a woman warrior named Kassondra in the country of Ektarr. She was the only person who could slay the Beast, a feat in which she succeeded admirably.

Now, Kassondra is becoming aware that her powers and presence are needed on BOTH sides of the time portal.

Draggon watched as Kassondra approached with her children.

Something was different.she had a resolute, purposeful stride and there was determination in her eyes. Had there been a new threat? Was she preparing for another battle he hadn't heard about yet?

Kassondra spoke gently to her old enemy/now friend.

"We've been through so much together, Draggon. We've aggravated each other, saved each other-now, I think it's time we found a place of solace, a place of safety where we can raise our children in peace."

Draggon felt twinges of happiness and apprehension at the same time.

She continued, "I've found such a place. Be here in one hour with your family and we'll go through the portal to safety together."

Draggon quickly checked his appearance and drew himself up to full size, preparing to speak with his children.

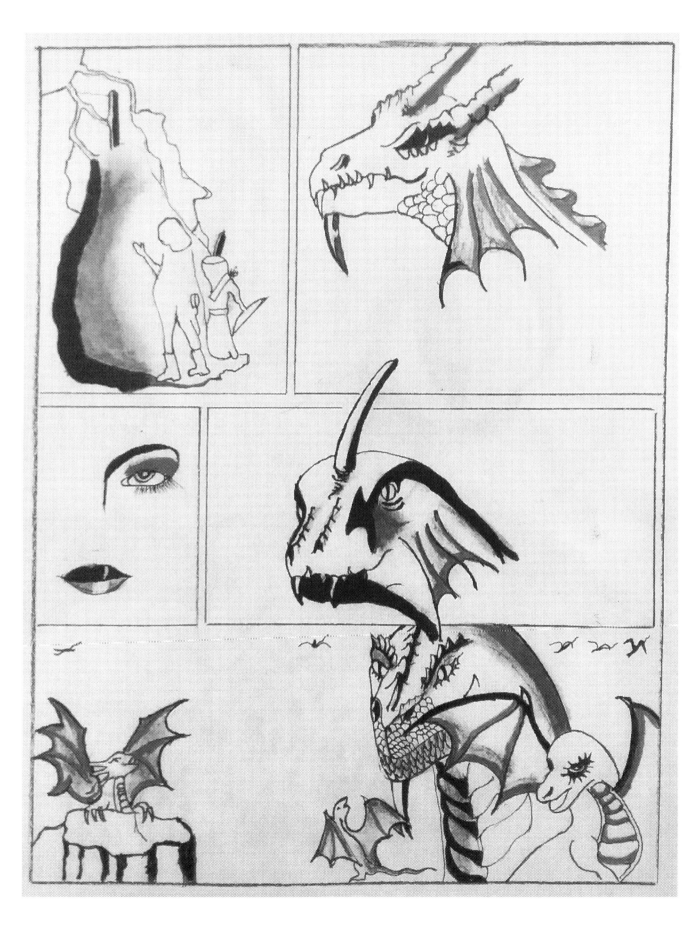

Draggon's children agree that it's best to move on.

Kassondra assures Draggon that NOW is the time and he is doing the right thing for his family.

"Gather all your friends, Draggon. Some may not want to join us, but give them the chance."

Within a second, all those who had gathered with Draggon and Kassondra were transported to the woods of Ektarr causing a loud sonic boom.

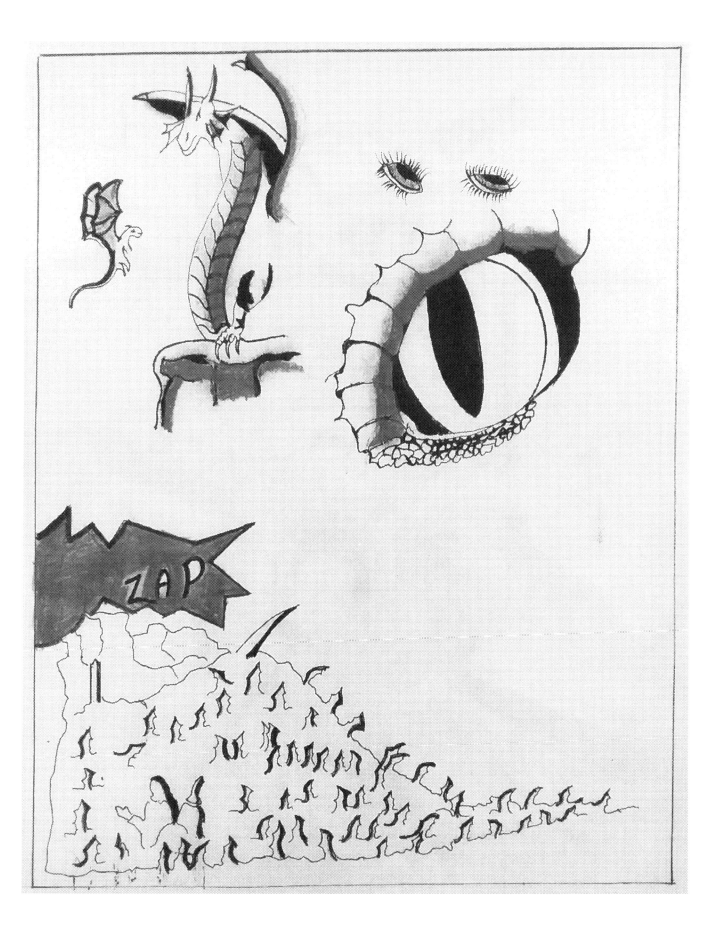

Kassondra/Rebecca tells everyone to remain in the woods while she deals with Caspian, the Wizard.

The townspeople, who had gathered to investigate the boom, began searching for Caspian. With shouts and screams, they call to him, unsure of Kassondra's intent. Was she there to harm them? Would there be a battle? Could Caspian save them if she tried to destroy them?

Soon, there was a general panic in the crowd.

Caspian hears the commotion and senses the volatile situation.

"I'm going to have to face her down and retrieve the sword," he thinks. "She's completed her quest, I must get the sword back now."

He prepared himself for a confrontation.

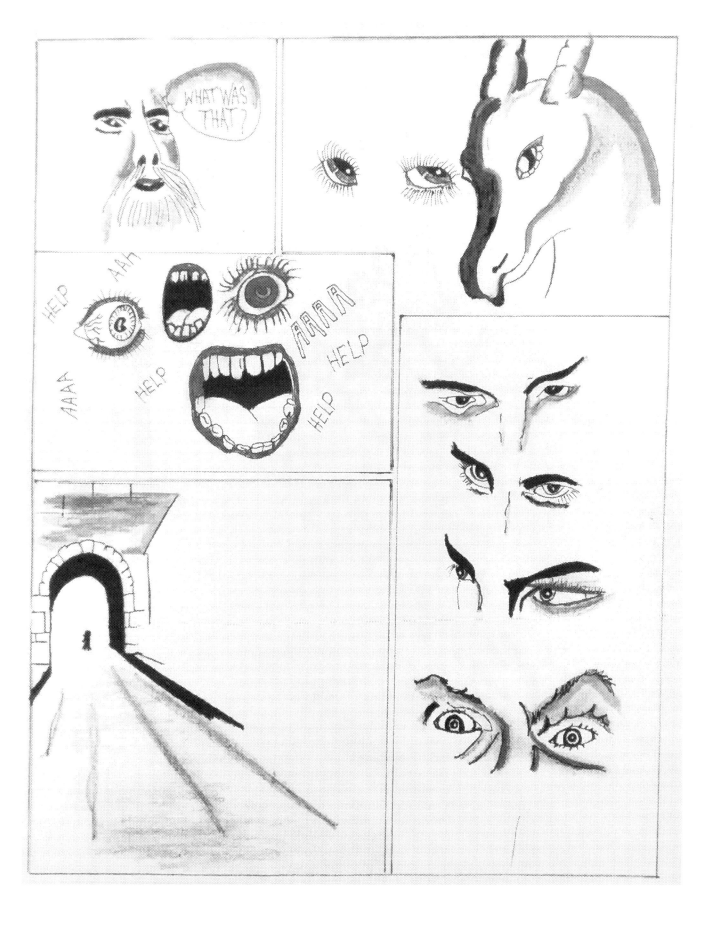

He approaches Kassondra carefully.

"Kassondra, how lovely to see you. I see you've brought the sword. That means you've succeeded in your quest. It's time, now, to return the sword to me."

"Yes, my quest is finished. I know you want the sword back," she agrees. Kassondra puts the sword into the ground between them and steps back. She waits for Caspian to take the bait. She has learned something about the sword that Caspian doesn't know. If he touches it...

Caspian bends over the sword and smiles. "The Book says the sword is mine!"

As Caspian touches the sword, an electrical charge throws him backward.

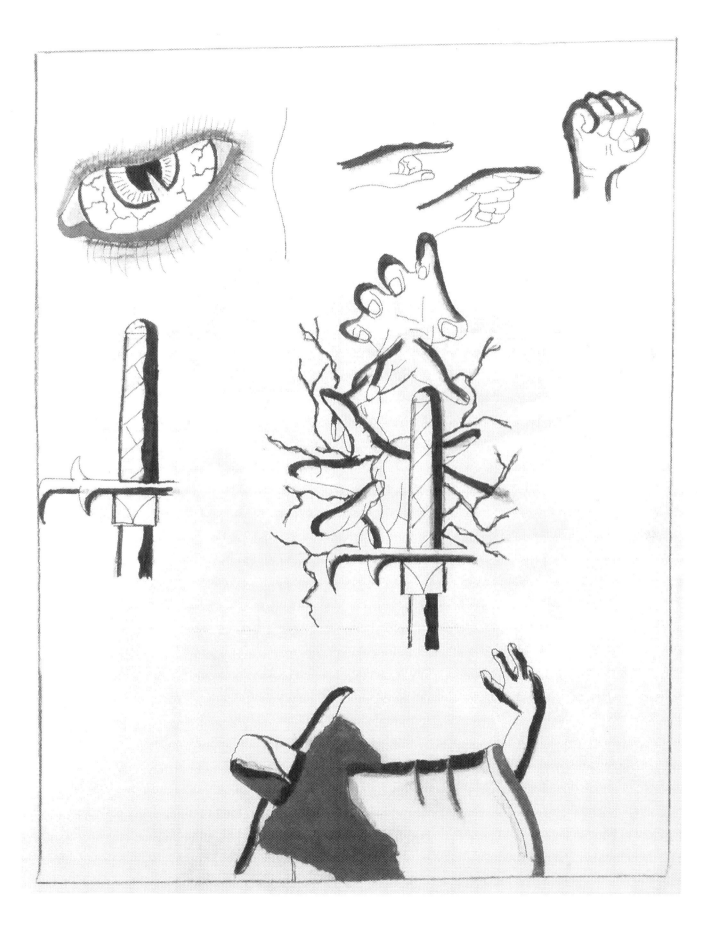

"WHY!? Why are you doing this?" he shouts. "The sword belongs to me now!"

Kassondra faces off with Caspian and puts all of her power into the Sword of Ektarr.

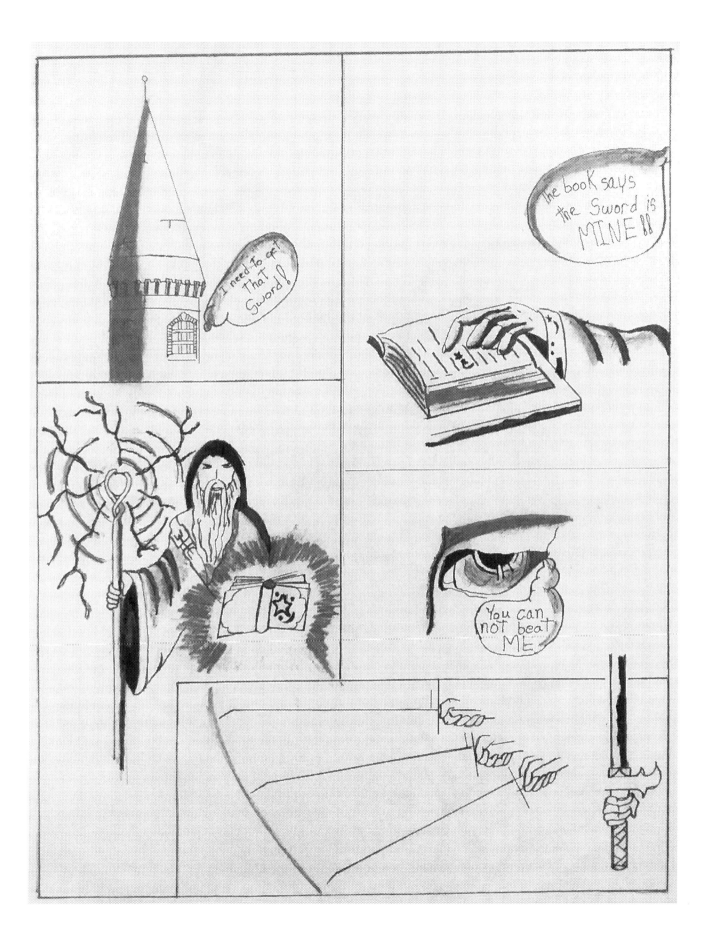

The Battle to end All Battles is about to begin.

Caspian -circles Kassondra cautiously. "I will ALWAYS have more power than you, Kassondra. Give it up! Give me the sword...I'm summoning my power NOW!"

Kassondra sneers, "That's all you have?!"

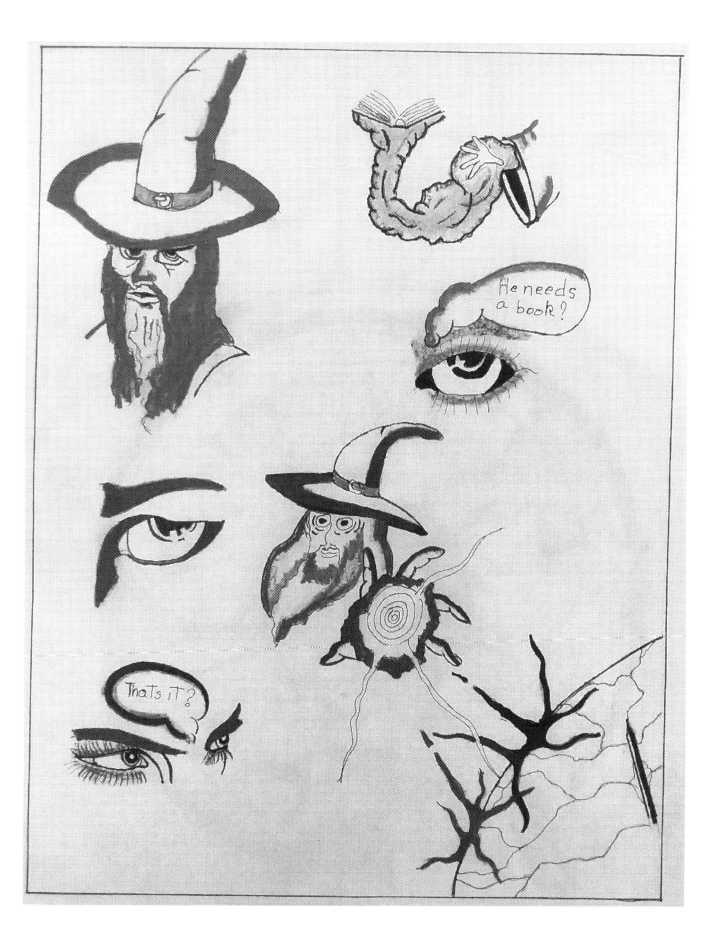

They exchange blows and magical thrusts of power. The battle goes on and on.

Kassondra sighs. "Caspian, we can do this all day...give me your best shot!"

Caspian summons all his power and throws what he thinks will be the final blow.

Kassondra falls to the ground.

"I told you that you cannot beat me!" he roars angrily.

Draggon, who had been watching from Caspian's castle tower, flies to Kassondra's rescue---

---but Caspian was ready for him. Throwing a fireball at the dragon, Caspian laughs as Draggon, badly hurt, hurtles to the ground.

The fireball hit Draggon square in the mouth and he hits the ground with a killing impact.

Kassondra regains her strength and is ready for another round.

Caspian shouts, "Are you ready to give up the sword NOW?" Kassondra pulls herself together and faces the Wizard. "NEVER!" she screams.

They circle each other ominously, each planning how to deliver a fatal blow to the other.

Kassondra realizes she has to get close to Caspian to kill him, and remembers that the last dragon she killed gave her sword the power of invisibility. Now she would use that to her advantage.

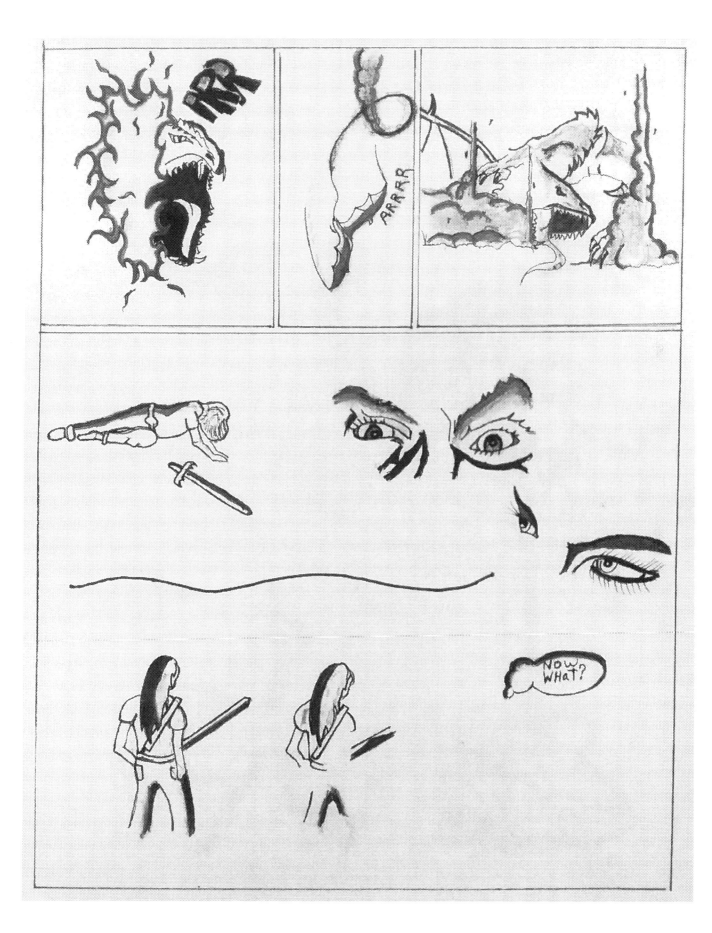

Caspian knows it will take only one more fireball to finish her off!

Unaware of the invisibility power the sword now possesses, Caspian makes his move as Kassondra uses the sword's most destructive powers!

Caspian falls to the ground, a mangled heap. Kassondra has no other choice but to end the battle. With tears in her eyes, she thrusts the sword into Caspian's chest.

As life leaves, his body evaporates. Now the sword gains even more power as it absorbs Caspian's abilities and magical ways.

Now, the Sword of Ektarr has more power than it needs.

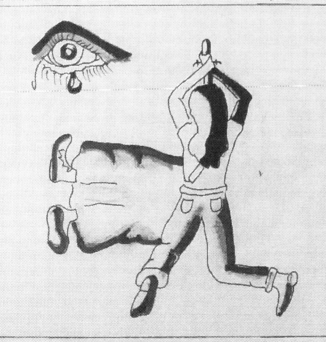

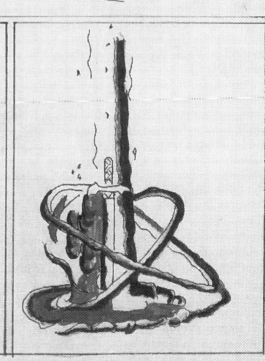

Kassondra is unaware that Draggon had sped to her rescue and fallen as a result of Caspian's blow.

Hearing the cried of the baby dragons, Kassondra hurries to the woods where she left them. Their cries put fear in her heart...something has happened to Draggon! She searches for him frantically!

Kassondra applies the healing powers of the sword to her friend and realizes that the waves of power are different, react faster and provide better results. She understands that the sword has inherited all the powers of Caspian.

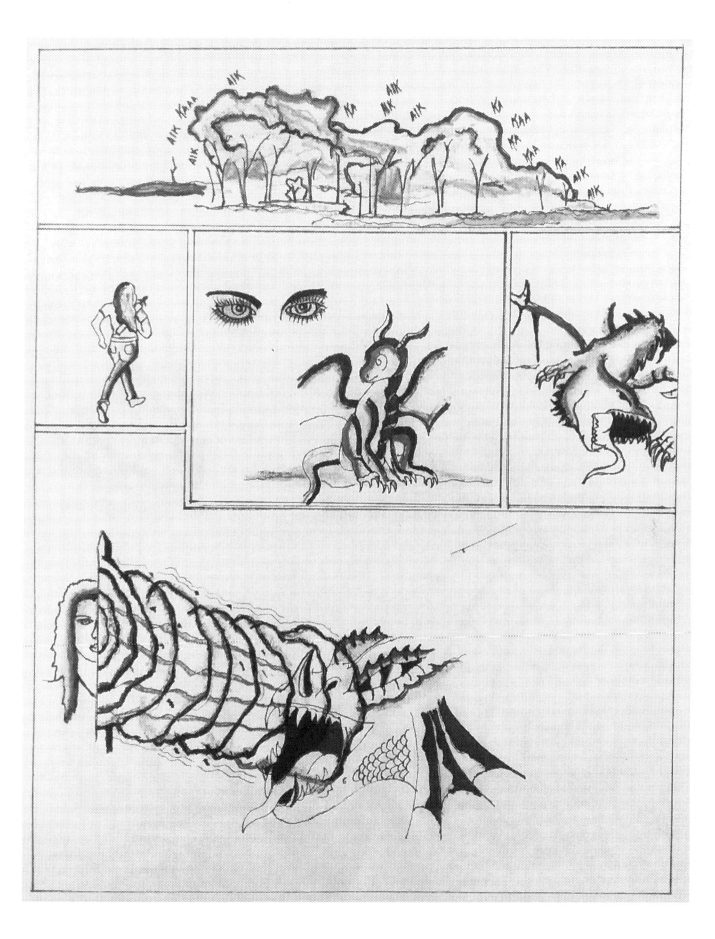

Rebecca gives each of her children a piece of the sword that she needs to return to the sight of her first encounter with the sword--Triple Peaks.

Draggon is now an experienced warrior and prepares himself for what he anticipates is to come. Covering himself with scales that are stronger than steel, he believes his armor is complete and that he is ready for the next battle.

Sadly, neither of them could know what awaited them at Triple Peaks.

The more Kassondra explains about Triple Peaks and the sword, the angrier Draggon becomes.

Suddenly...

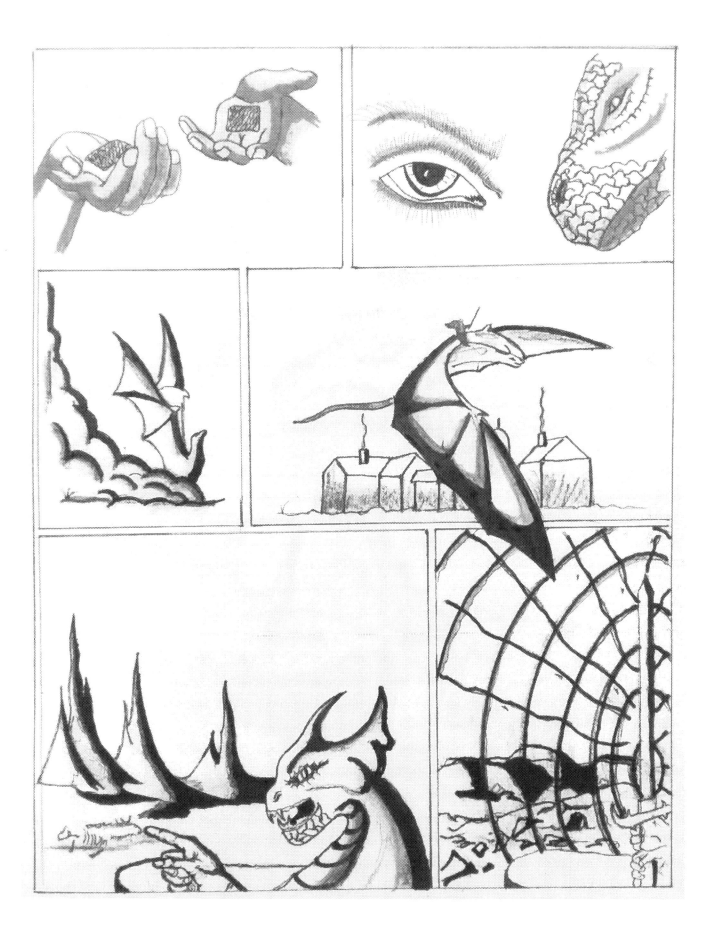

...Kassondra is aware that her children are in trouble. She and Draggon speed to the site.

"That is one BIG dragon!" Draggon gasps.

Kassondra frowns. "Yeah, he's a big one-but the big fall hard! He must have come through with us when we left your world, Draggon."

Kassondra sighs. Another fight is about to take place.

Torrance, the dragon, explains that he is thankful that he was given the opportunity to get out of his world of constant strife and danger.

"Now that I'm in this realm, I will rule supreme!"

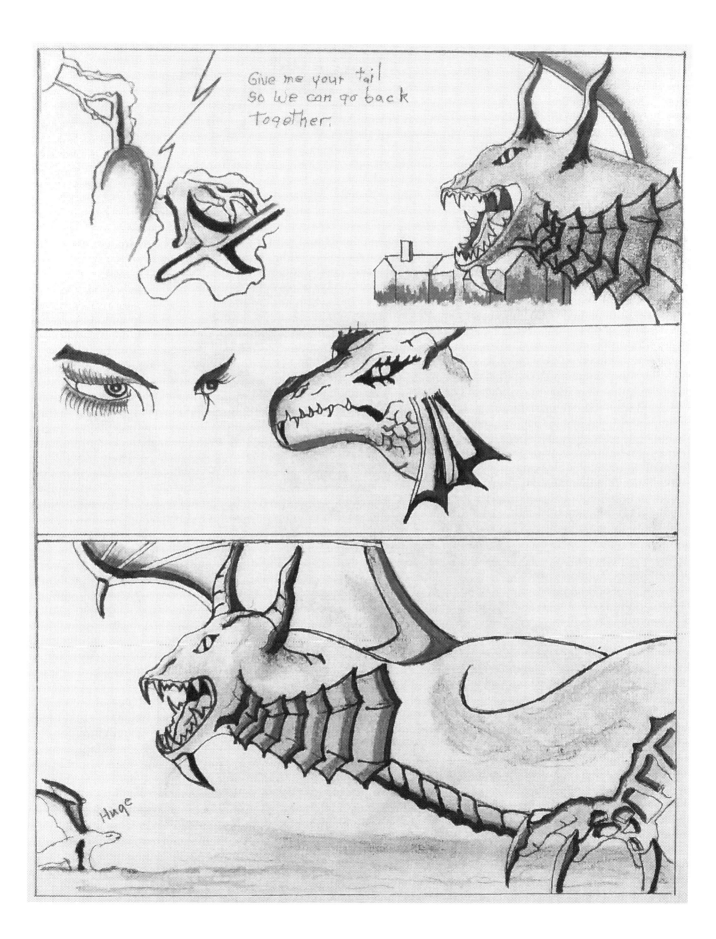

Kassondra steps in front of Draggon. "'Let me take care of Torrance. You stay out of it."

Torrance chides Draggon. "Come on, baby dragon. Let's see what you've got."

Before Kassondra could stop him, Draggon is in the air, facing off with Torrance. The attack is so swift that Kassondra has no change to defend Draggon!

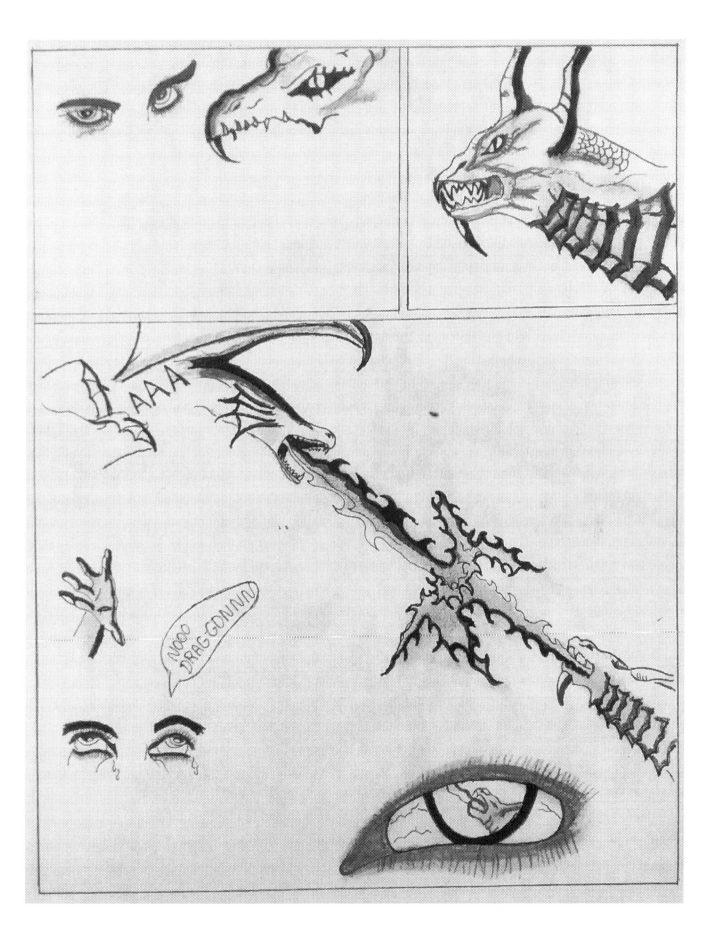

$\mathcal{W}$ith absolutely no time to spare, Kassondra uses the Sword of Ektarr to end the fight.

The two warriors are joined by their children, who frolic around the body of the giant dragon from another world.

Draggon and Kassondra decide that it would be wise to check throughout the land to see if any other intruders followed them through the portal.

Satisfied that the giant was the only intruder, Kassondra begins her search for the castle. She finds the Wizards' lair, where the sacred book is kept.

Reading through the pages, she finds that Caspian was speaking the truth when he said she must return the sword to him at the completion of her quest.

But she couldn't hand it over to a mad man, and she felt that the quest was not truly over yet. Now, with the sacred book she was even more powerful. This was a thrilling thought, but also ominous. She would have to control herself or she would end up like Caspian.

The more she thought about it, the more she realized that she must ultimately destroy the book..

*K*assondra builds a cabinet to protect the sword, and expected some kind of reaction-a mystical event of some kind, as she had experienced when handling the sword in the past.

But there was none.

Nothing at all. Slightly confused-and a bit disappointed-she turns to Caspian's belongings to, perhaps, make things clearer to her.

As she goes through Caspian's things, she realizes that the Book and the sword are both still active, and she began to feel that this was where she belonged.

Sitting with her children, she tried to explain that this would be their new home. She told them how she had hurt the soldiers in their world and would not be welcomed back.

"But this this is a wonderful place!" she whispered. "Here we will never grow old; here, there are dragons! Kind, but powerful dragons. Perhaps one day, if you're gentle and kind, one will let you ride through the sky on his back!"

The children nod in excitement.

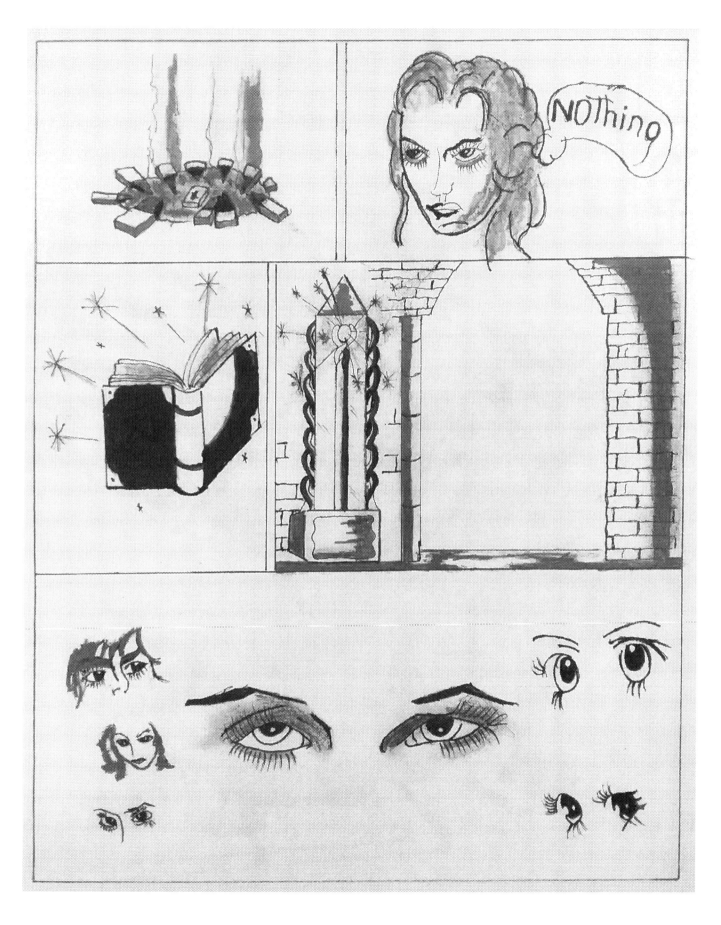

Continuing her search for something to lead her to the next step, she finds a staff and more scrolls.

She discovers that Ektarr is protected in a radius of 150 miles by a magical dome powered by the book and the staff. Upon further investigation, she arrives at the alchemy lab. The scrolls tell her that only a person that has the magic of Ektarr may pass through the barrier.

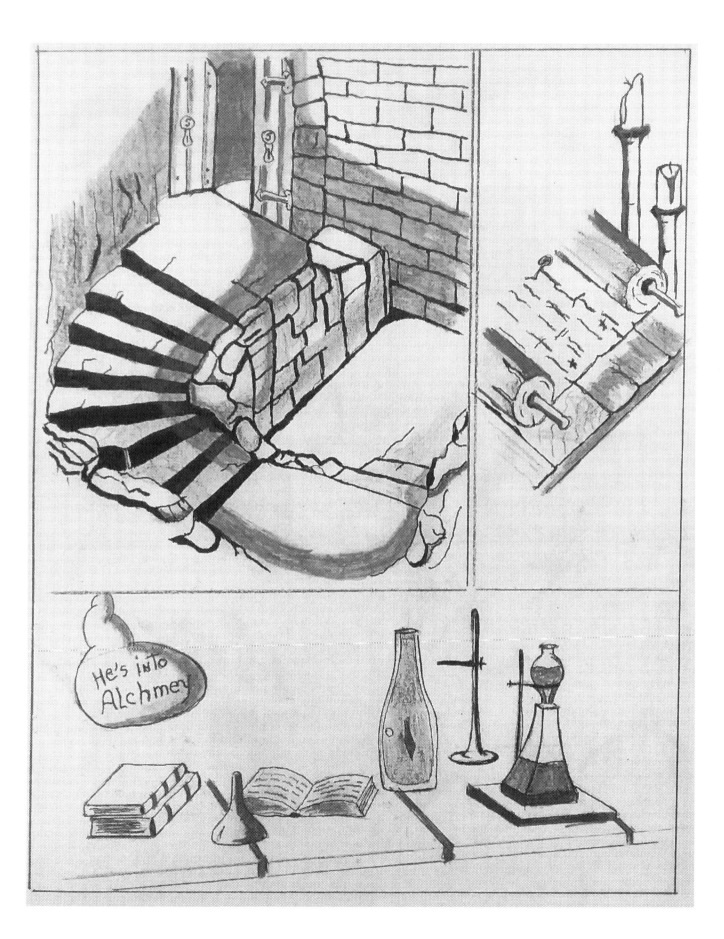

Understanding now that she must insure the safety of her family and that of Draggon's, she decides that she must change the dome shield-make it stronger, less able to penetrate by enemies.

In the Book of All Wizards, she finds the words and reinforces the dome so that only one who holds the sword or staff of Ektarr can enter. She extends the field of protection to a 200 mile radius and 5 miles vertically. Aware that this process will take twelve hours to complete, she worries that predators may be lurking in the kingdom who had entered before the shield was reinforced.

Draggon and his friends patrol the land for a period of two weeks, searching for any sign of trouble or danger.

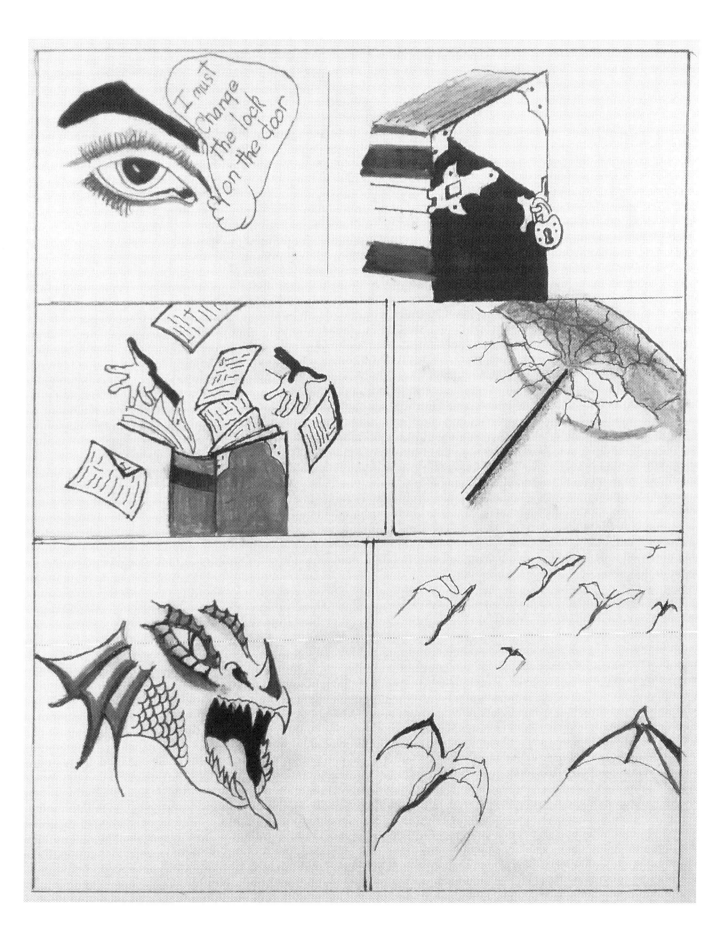

Draggon spots a strange creature standing outside the protective shield.

He flies down to get a better look. What kind of creatures ARE these? More are gathering, but they can't get in.

Draggon wonders if some may have entered before the shield was reinforced and calls Kassondra.

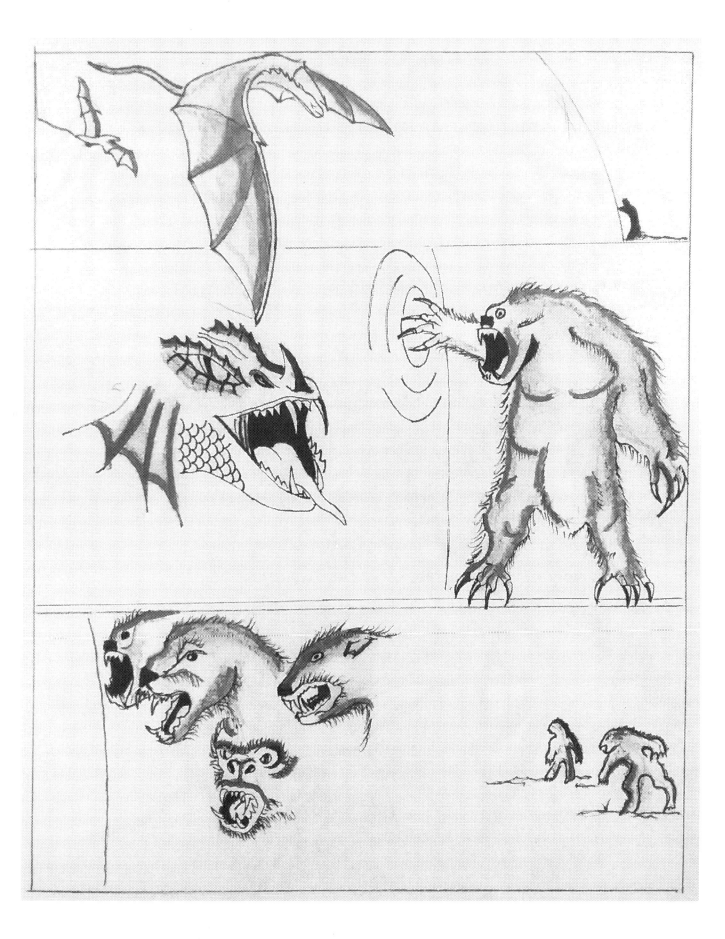

Kassondra interrupts her study of the Book of All Wizards and transports to the site.

The creatures are 15 feet tall and look vicious.

"They can't get in, Draggon, but I wonder if any entered before the shield was completely sealed. Check again."

Draggon spots a group of 20 creatures by the river.

Kassondra and Draggon quickly destroy the herd.

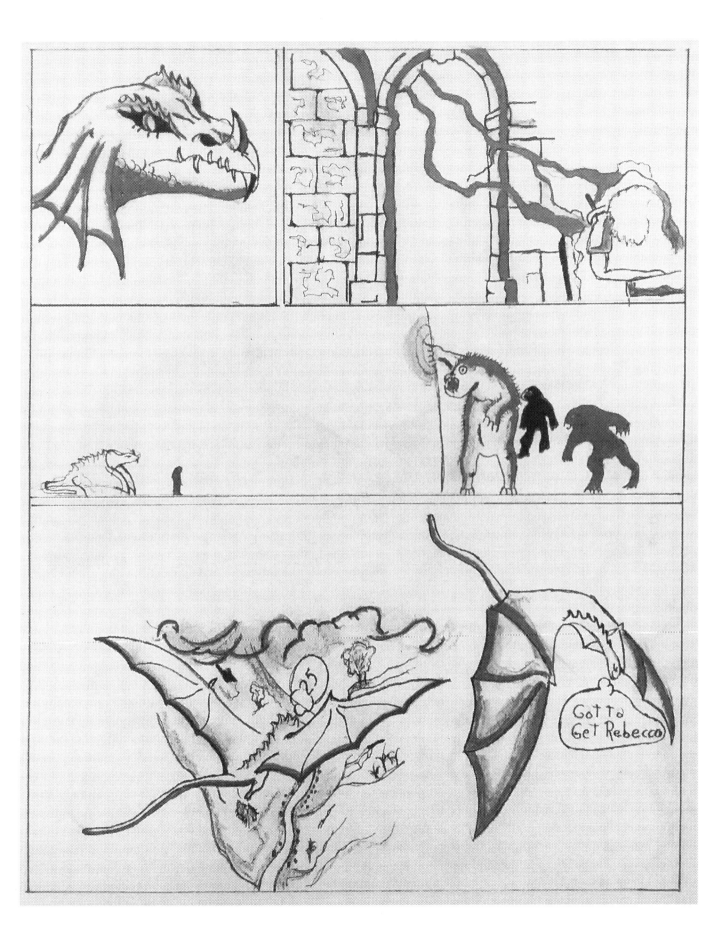

Talking to a few villagers and the mayor, Kassondra learns that there are no animals in the land.

"The people must have a reason to live, to love Ektarr. We must make them self-sufficient, give them pride in themselves, and a purposeful life."

So Kassondra and Draggon return to Rebecca's world and return with 2000 cows, 2000 chickens, and 200 horses. She transports enough grain to .let the animals survive until the residents of Ektarr can establish farms and grow crops.

The people are motivated and begin changing their lifestyle. Excited, they eagerly anticipate a better life to come.

Kassondra, still curious about <u>her</u> existence and purpose, keeps searching the books and scrolls for information.

She discovers why the wizard's scroll is so important.

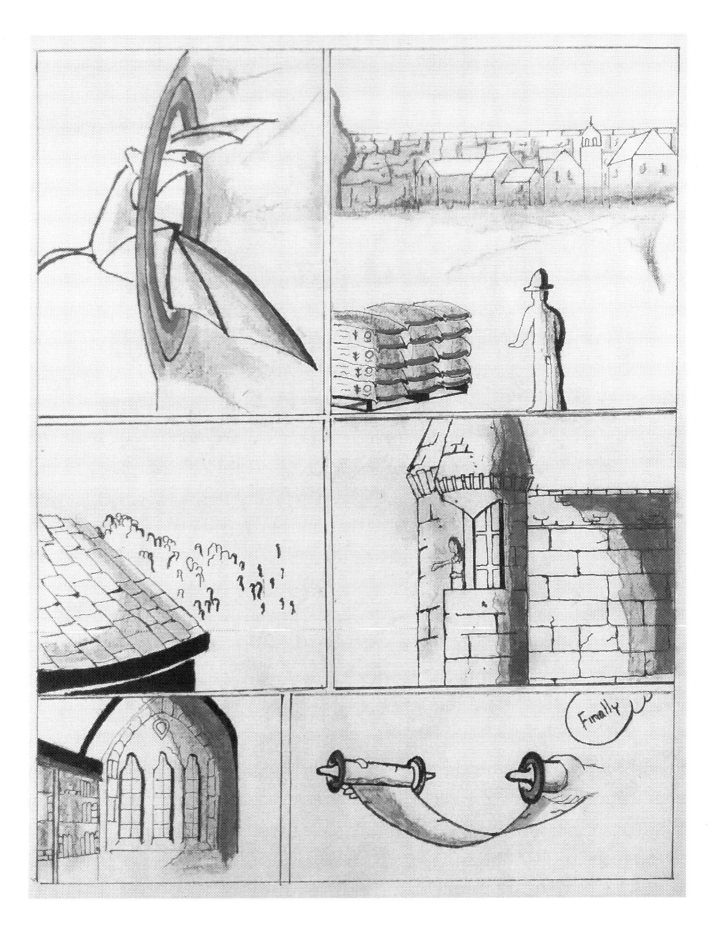

Kassondra wonders if she has the power to summon the other two wizards. The books and scrolls speak of three wizards and she has known only Caspian thus far.

Wondering what they will be like, she summons the wizards.

From The Time of De-sin, three gr
wizards left to have a good life.
only one returned. While despe
wanting a different Life. Kasson
Maybe I can Summons the Other Two Wizards
WHO HAS THE POWER TO Summons ME?

"I wanted to see all the wizards, so I summoned you.

"YOU are one, I am the second, and Caspian was number three," Comdities responds.

Kassondra smiles. "I just wanted to meet you face-to-face."

"OK, you've met me. Now let's get something straight: this cannot be shared. You may be my assistance," Comdities replies.

Kassondra smiles even wider. "That will not happen!"

Comdities strokes his beard. "Well, if you are not willing to share the power, I will simply take it from you."

Draggon, sensing that a fight is about to occur, readies his armor.

As Comdities and Kassondra face off.
From nowhere, Torade comes forth and spews fire.

Torade. rains fire on monsters.

Kassondra, growing bored with the fight, invokes her invisibility and ends the conflict with Comdities.

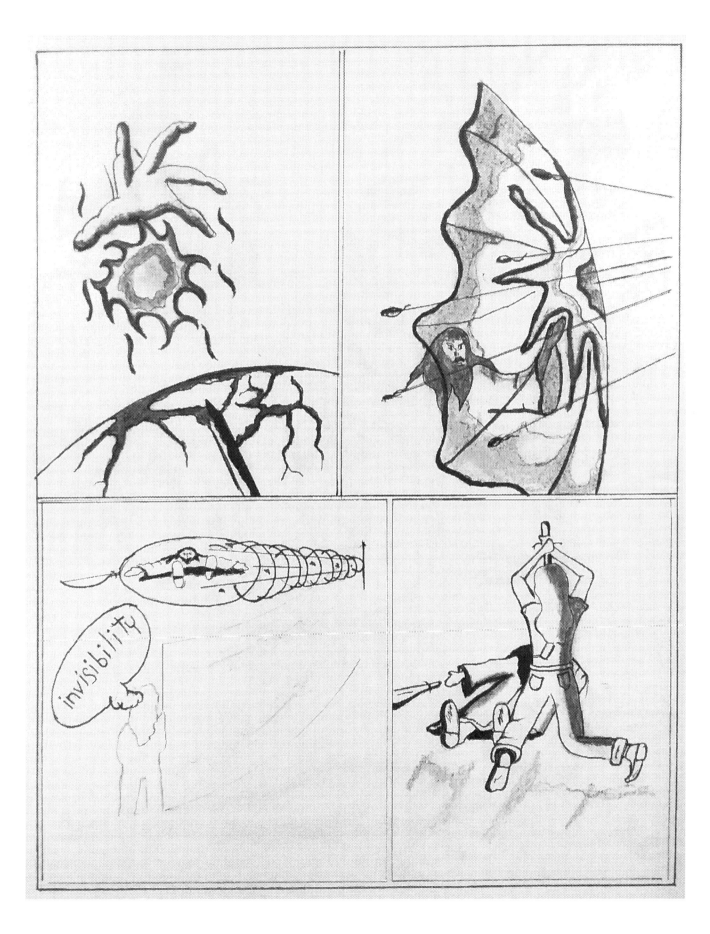

Kassondra, victorious once again, feels confident and powerful. Could I someday return to my world? She wonders.

Little does she know that her world is on stand-by.

Returning with Draggon to gather food for Ektarr, Kassondra is wary.

F84s scramble to their targets, but experience no confrontations.

Controlling time and space, Kassondra places the F84s back on their airfield, as if they'd never left.

She and Draggon continue toward the food warehouse.

Speaking to the Flight Commander, Captain Rogers complains, "Sir, nother work on the jets! They are totally dead. It has to be that woman and her dragon. We can't compete·with her magical sword!"

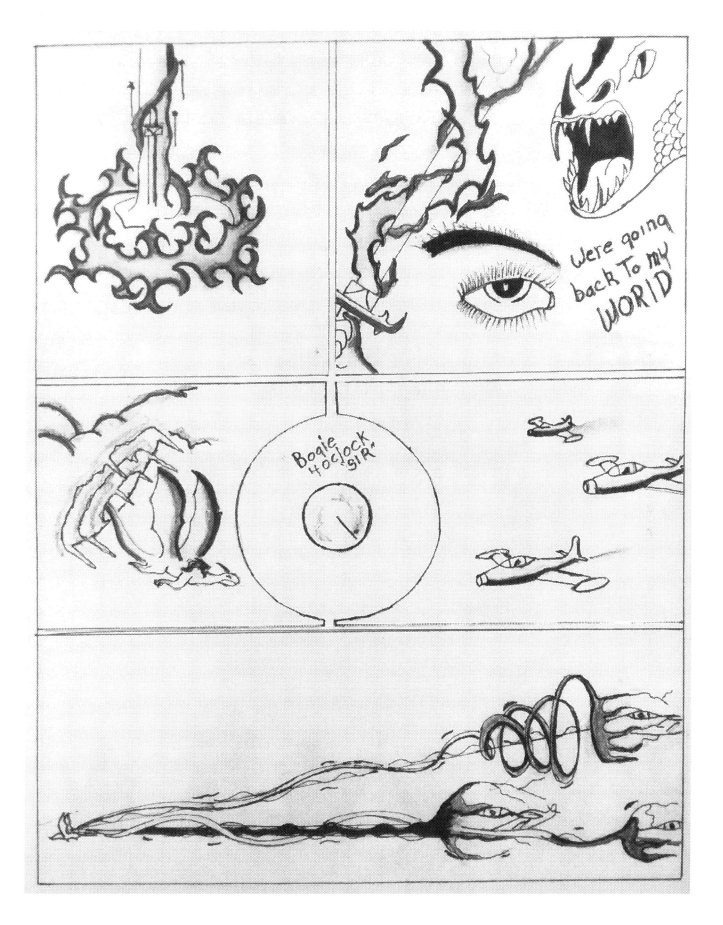

The Flight Commander thinks. "Maybe she just wants food for her people. I'm fine with that. She put the fighters back on the field without harming them. Maybe she isn't here to hurt anyone."

Pacing, he continues. "There has to be a way to contact her, some way to get in touch. Can we leave messages in the food warehouse? What do we say? We need some sort of agreement, a treaty, a truce..."

"We are powerless against her magic, her cosmic strength. That's what we need to get... an agreement that she will use her power FOR us and not against us!"

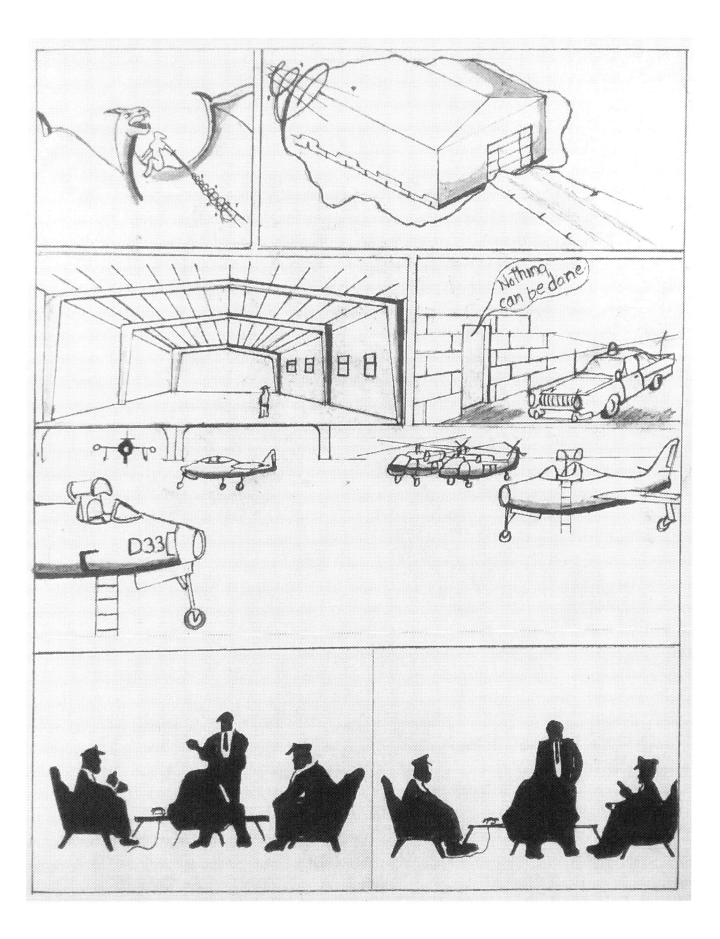

Dugon, not realizing that Caspian is dead, decides to practice hls usual mischief, frightening the citizens. As Caspian's favorite torture machine, he has always had free reign.

Kassondra discovers his plan. "This has to stop, Dugon."

Draggon frowns, "You must leave, Dugon. You have no place here anymore."

Dugon becomes defiant. "I won't leave! Not without a fight! Caspian and I are masters here. It's YOU who don't belong!"

Draggon shakes his head. "Not anymore, Dugon. Caspian is DEAD!"

Draggon, unaware of Dugon's full power, takes his best shot, but is no match for Dugon.

Seeing Draggon go down makes Kassondra angry.

"THIS ENDS NOW, DUGON!"

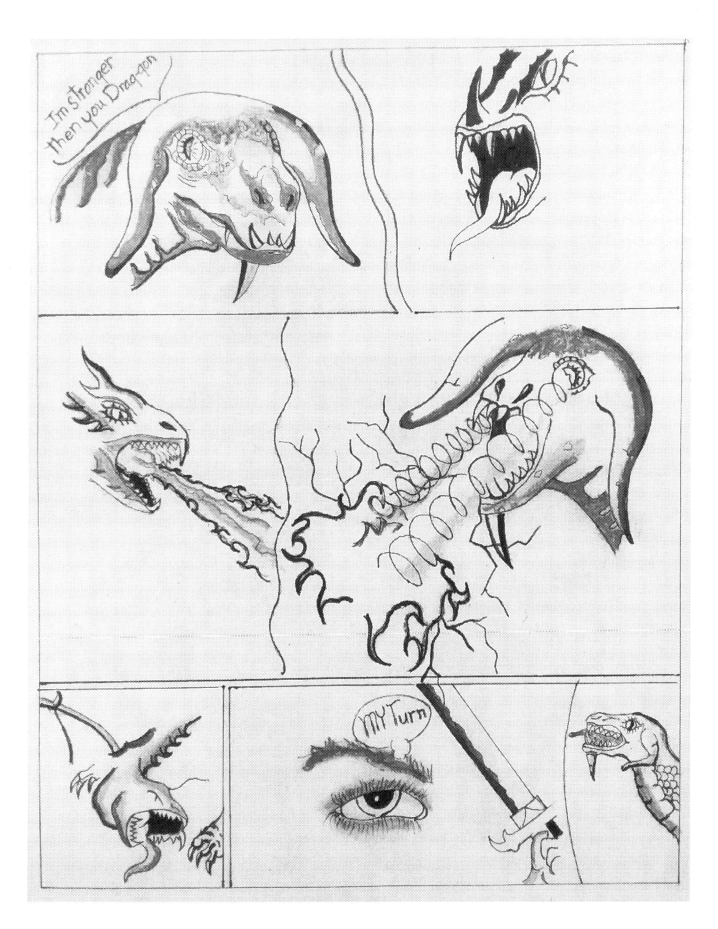

$\mathcal{M}$eanwhile--

"General, as Mayor, I'm telling you, we have to do something about this woman!"

"Well, Ektarr has no phone system. The scientists tell me she's in a different dimension. You know, like Einstein wrote about."

The Mayor persists. "So how do we contact her?"

"The only thing I can think of is to put messages in the food warehouse, let her go in, and hope she finds them."

So this was done.

The battle with Dugon continued. Draggon lay on the ground. Kassondra sensed that something was about to happen-something had.

"Dugon, go! Go· • • • - ••, '· and be safe. Go • .....and LIVE!"

Dugon screams at her, "NEVER!"

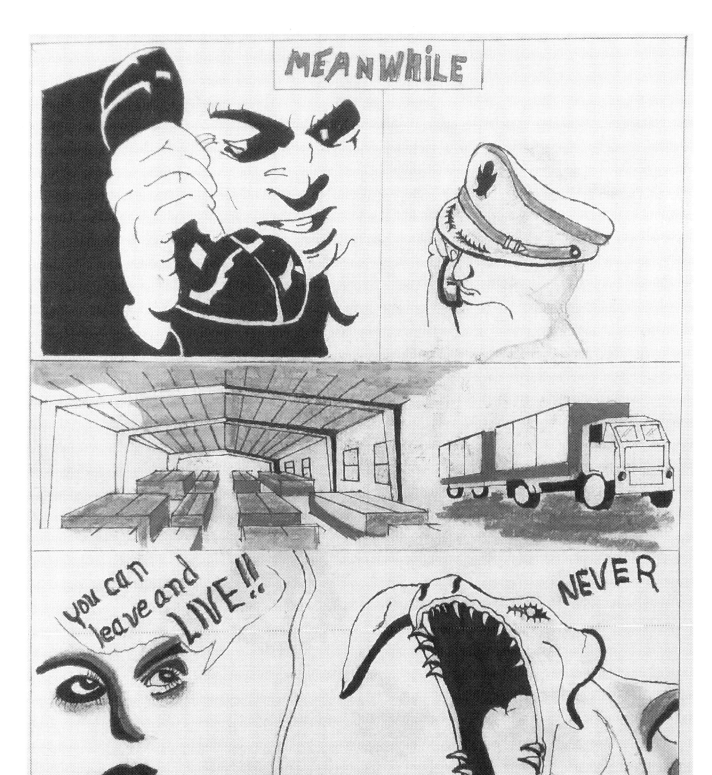

Dugon, more angry than ever at hearing that his glory days as master were over, hits Kassondra with all his might.

Kassondra prepares herself for the worst. She thinks his rage is coming from fear and wonders if she can frighten him into submission.

Dugon .circles Kassondra. "What are you doing?"

"Can't you see? I'm reviving Draggon," Kassondra replies.

Dugon sneers. "No single wizard can do that." "No, but THREE CAN," Kassondra shouts. "Three? I don't see three wizards!"

"Dugon, it's all in the sword. Think!"

Suddenly Dugon understands. The power of the three wizards resides in the sword now, and Kassondra's statement, "Leave and live!" was a warning to him. Knowing that the sword can destroy him, he speaks frantically.

"But where do I go if I leave here? Is there a place for me? What shall{do?

Kassondra looks into his eyes. "I will put you under a 100 mile dome, away from here. No one will be able to get in or out. You'll be safe. You'll live! You have three days, Dugon! DECIDE."

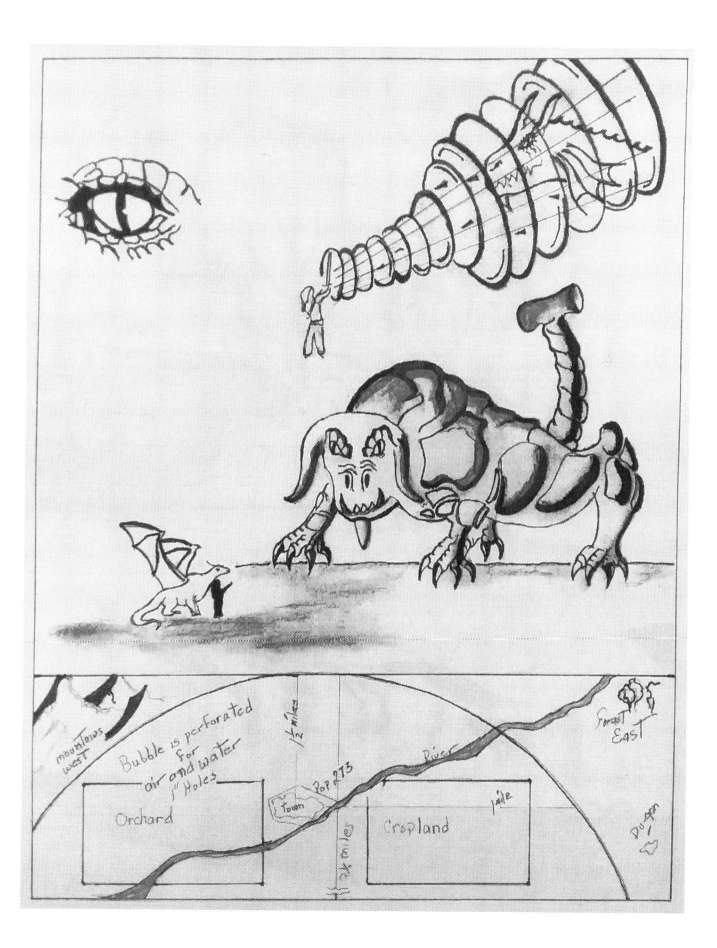

Dugon picks three possible sites that look promising.

Because he can't fly, he asks Draggon to help.

Dugon is now ready to leave and be content with safety and long life.

Kassondra and Draggon relax in the knowledge that there will be -no more fighting.

Warning her children to keep the chips of her sword close to them, Kassondra turns to Draggon.

"Well, as master, I'm going to need a dragon. I need a ride, Draggon."

Draggon smiles. "I thought you'd never ask!"

In his heart, he knows that every time he's gone with Kassondra there has been trouble, so he keeps him armor on.

"I'm so lucky to be a shape-shifter!" he thinks to himself. "What is THAT?" Draggon asks.

Kassondra smiles, "That, my friend, is a tyrannosaurus rex, but don't worry about him. You have flight and fire. He has only teeth and feet!"

*A*yrmosseth flies out of the clouds. Draggon hears her. Kassondra tells him to get her, but not to harm her.

"Tell her a female wants to talk with her!" Kassondra shouts.

As Ayrmosseth and Kassondra talk, and Kassondra gives her the protection of the dome.

"What about the other two?" Draggon asks.

'They are males and will want to dominate their own worlds. They are not ready to share our world. It's a male thing, Draggon."

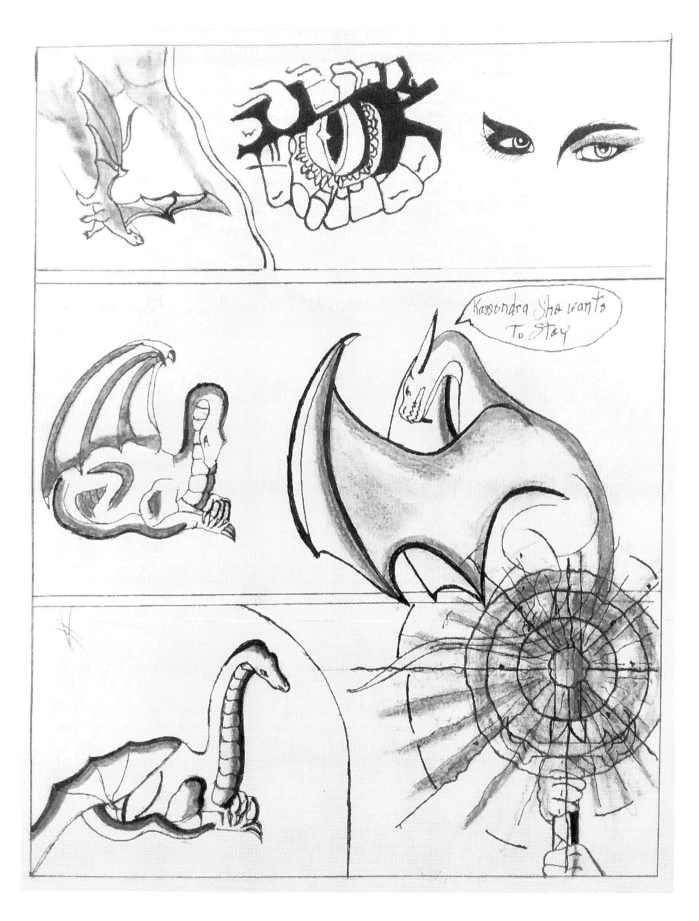

Kassondra returns to the Wizards' Conference Room to contemplate.

Her world was almost perfect now. Looking at the village below, she suddenly realizes, "I would like to have a Clock Tower!"

So she returns to her world.

*A*fter she took the clocks, she put them in the Tower of Ektarr and explained time to the residents.

Feeling exuberant now, she begins to think about her beginning. "I think I'll go to De-Sin," she thinks. "According to what I've read, that's where I'm from."

She calls Draggon.

"Draggon, you need a protective dome, too," she says, and makes it happen.

Draggon and Kassondra are now ready to fly off to De-Sin.

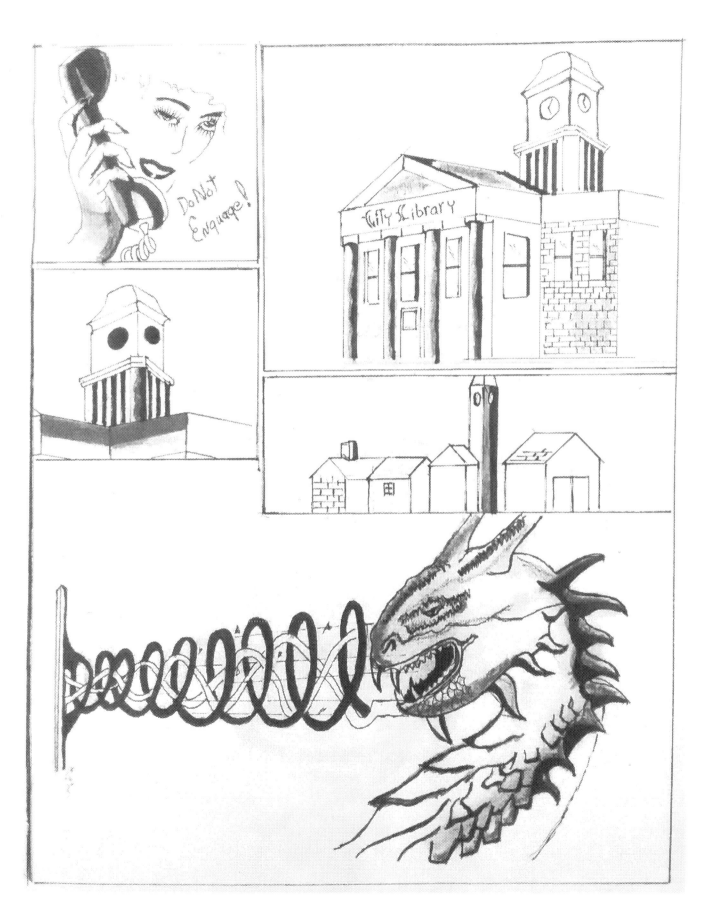

Ahriman lives in De-Sin and he is reluctant to face her. He stands with his minions.

They are no match for Kassondra. Ahriman hides in his lair, letting the others do his fighting.

"You talk strange," he shouts from his lair. "Explain your word 'scruples'."

Kassondra smiles. "You wouldn't understand. Come out and face me. Did you understand that?"

"I don't need to face you. I don't know you. What is your name?"

Kassondra patiently replies, "Kassondra."

"I know you," Ahriman replies. "You were of this land." "I was, but it wasn't this bad when I was here before." "So why did you come back?"

"To clean the land of garbage." ·

Ahriman shakes his head. "Again, I don't understand the word 'garbage'." Kassondra smiles. "You will."

Ahriman responds, "You don't have the power. No wizard does."

Kassondra answers, "I took it from Comdities and Caspian. Their powers are in my sword now. Take your minions and leave this town."

So they left and Kassondra put a protective dome over the town.

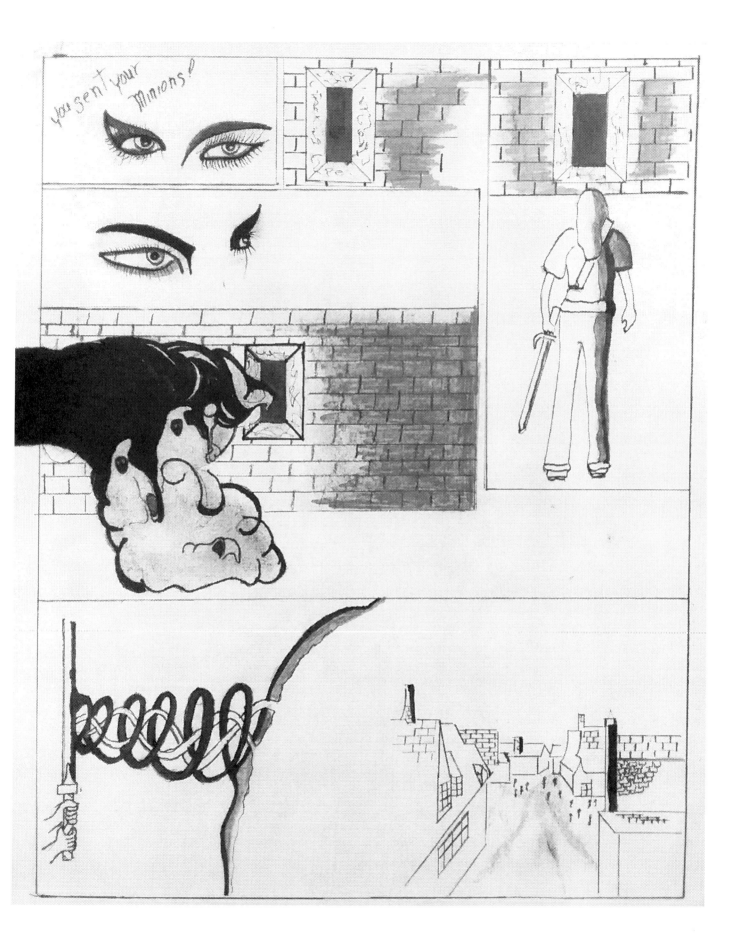

Kassondra tells the one she chose to be governor that she will be the overseer of the land, and will not tolerate anything that goes against the te ching of the laws in the Book.

She gives the governor a piece of the sword and explains its power.

Before leaving De-Sin, Kassondra and Draggon destroy the dungeon where Draggon was kept prisoner.

Draggon is filled with joy to leave this place of bad memories and soars into the air with the power of an F84, creating a whirlwind on the ground.

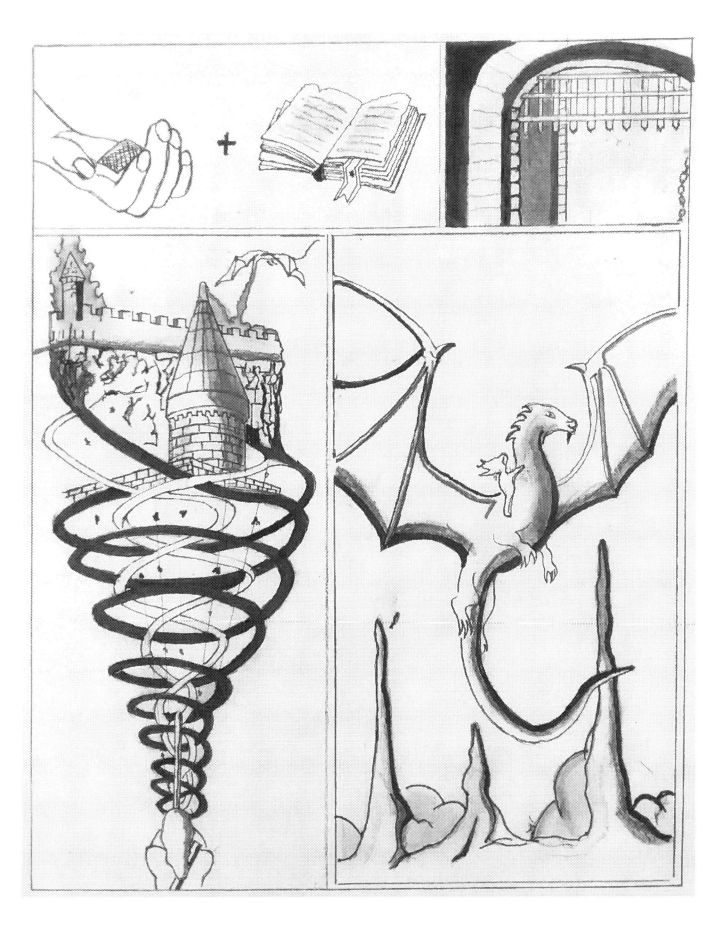

$\mathcal{K}$assondra returns to her studies of the book and the scrolls and discovers that 50 years have passed in her world.

Draggon speaks, amazed, "But we haven't aged at all! Are you going there to see how things are now?

While deciding what to do next, an armada of alien creatures in assorted vehicles have entered Earth's atmosphere. NASA has known about the armada for a century and realize that these creatures take and destroy. They come from a star system years from Earth.

Earth has been preparing for this encounter, but their weapons will be weak compared to those of the aliens.

Here is another quest-another battle for Kassondra and Draggon-but they have not made the decision to return to Earth. Will they return and save the planet?

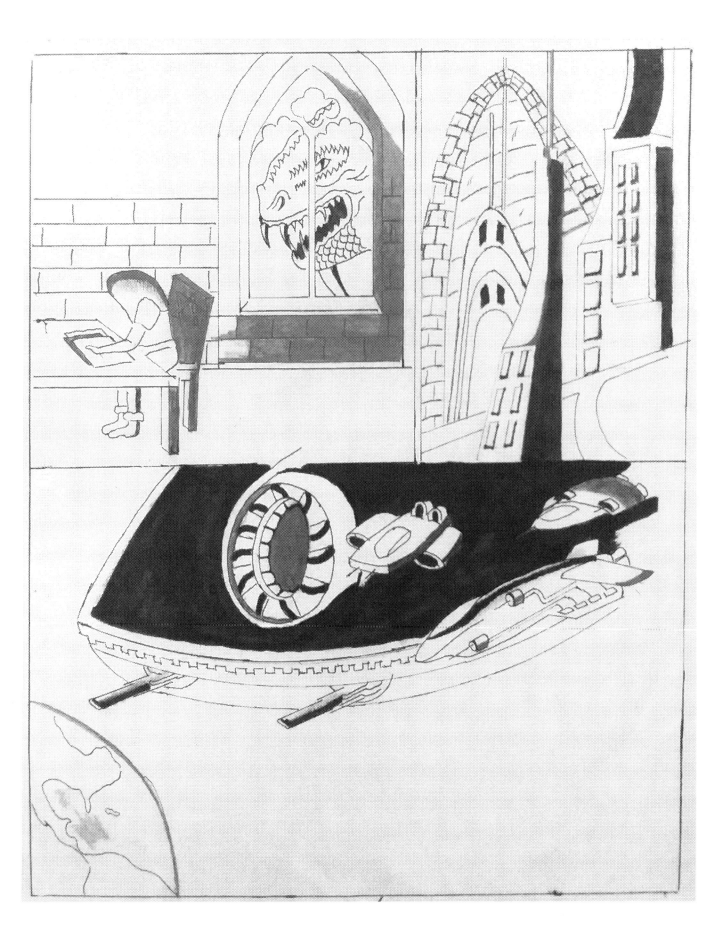

Printed in the United States
By Bookmasters